CREEPY CAVES

ELF GIRL and RAVEN BOY

CREEPY CAVES

ELF GIRL and RAVEN BOY

MARCUS SEDGWICK

Illustrated by Pete Williamson

Orion
Children's Books

First published in Great Britain in 2015
by Orion Children's Books
a division of the Orion Publishing Group Ltd
Orion House
5 Upper St Martin's Lane
London WC2H 9EA
An Hachette UK Company

1 3 5 7 9 10 8 6 4 2

Printed in Great Britain by CPI Group (UK) Ltd,
Croydon, CRO 4YY

www.orionbooks.co.uk

For Raven Boy and Elf Girl.

And Rat.

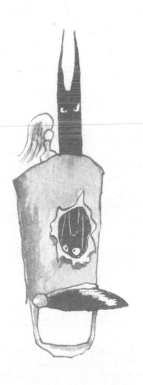

Scream
Sea

The Isla

Monster
Mountains

Fright Forest

Dread Desert

Terror Town

Creepy Caves

ONE

**Raven Boy has decided that if
they ever make it back home
in one piece he is going to
never do anything
brave again.**

'I think,' said Raven Boy, 'that I liked things
better when it was just the three of us.'

Rat squeaked in agreement, and Elf Girl
squeezed past three smelly and noisy trolls to
join Raven Boy at the edge of the flying carpet
on which they were travelling.

Raven Boy was lying on his front, chin
on the rug, staring at the landscape whizzing by
underneath them. He held a sword to one side

of him. Rat sat on top of his head. Elf Girl dangled her feet over the side.

'I know what you mean,' she said.

The carpet, whose name was Shona, was trying to keep order on her flight. It was the busiest she'd been since she'd become a flying carpet, and all in all she had eight passengers on board.

First and second, there were Raven Boy and Elf Girl. You might know something about them already. Raven Boy is the scruffy one with feathers in his hair and

a tatty black coat. Elf Girl is the one with pointy boots and even pointier ears, ears that go pink when she gets cross, something which happens fairly often.

Then there was Rat; their constant companion, usually found hiding in one of Raven Boy's pockets, except if there's a whiff of food around, in which case he'll be hunting for it straight away.

Fourth, fifth and sixth were the three smelly trolls, whose names were Bert, Bob and Cedric. Bert was the smallest one, and the smartest, though that's not saying very much, because Bob, the middle-sized one, and Cedric, the large one, were both as dumb as sleepy slugs.

They'd been trying to catch Raven Boy and Elf Girl ever since they met in Fright Forest, weeks ago. Catch them, and eat them, but for reasons that Elf Girl and Raven Boy weren't quite sure about, the trolls had recently agreed not to eat them until they found their way to the land of the Goblin King. Elf Girl wasn't convinced it was a good idea, especially as Raven Boy seemed to have agreed that the trolls could eat them once the Goblin King had been defeated. Elf Girl didn't think much of that part of the plan.

Then, seventh, there was Lord Socket, a rather snooty young ruler from Terror Town, the place they'd just left, and eighth, his magician, a funny old man called Klingsor, who kept muttering things under his beard that no one could quite understand.

It was Klingsor who'd gone into an odd kind of trance and announced that Raven Boy was the one person in the world who might be able to defeat the Goblin King. The magician had called Raven Boy the 'wise fool', which Raven Boy thought was a bit rude.

Still, they did have two more things on their side in their quest to defeat the evil Goblin King. The first was a bottle of water, known as the Tears of the Moon, which came from a magical oasis, and the second was the Singing Sword, which they guessed must be very dangerous if you knew how to use it. The only problem was that no one, not even Klingsor, knew how to use the tears or the sword to defeat the Goblin King.

In the meantime, the sword would keep rattling out cheesy love song after cheesy love song, living up to its name. It never stopped singing, absolutely never, unless Raven Boy had a hold of it, in which case it would fall silent, another strange thing which Klingsor said proved that Raven Boy was the chosen one; the one who could defeat the evil, powerful and utterly wicked Goblin King.

Socket and Klingsor were arguing about why Terror Town had got into the mess it got into, and the trolls were arguing about who was the smelliest. It seemed they all wanted to be the stinkiest. Shona the carpet was yelling at everyone, telling them to sit down while they were in flight, but no one was taking any notice of her. She was getting very cross indeed.

It was night. They'd decided to make the journey to the land of the Goblin King in the dark, so they wouldn't be spotted.

A big hungry moon hung overhead, shining down and showing them . . . not much.

'Look,' said Raven Boy, unhappily.

'It's a wasteland,' said Elf Girl.

'We must be getting close,' said Raven Boy, nodding. 'He's destroyed everything!'

That seemed to be true.

As the sun started to come up, the full horror of the landscape became clear.

They could see smouldering tree stumps where forests had once been; there were the ruins of houses and weed-choked streets where there had once been villages. They flew over rivers and streams that were black and looked as though they had been poisoned.

'Dawn's breaking,' Raven Boy called to Shona. 'We should find somewhere to land and hide until it's dark again.'

'No need,' said Elf Girl. 'I think we're there.'

She pointed ahead of the flying carpet.

In the distance was a pair of huge gates set into the ground and, as they flew closer, the gates turned out to be even larger than they had thought. It was obvious that they had come to the land of the Goblin King.

For one thing, the gates were carved into the forms of giant monstrous creatures, with

claws and horns and teeth. Lots of teeth.

And for another thing, the country beyond the gates was even more of a desolate wasteland.

They all fell silent; even the squabbling trolls, who, as soon as the sun came up, would turn back into men.

On the horizon, the land started to climb into a series of mountains; the most barren and scary-looking range of mountains any of them had ever seen.

Bert grunted.

'The Haunted Hills,' he said.

'Why do they always have such nice names?' sighed Raven Boy.

'And in the hills,' Bert went on, 'somewhere, is the entrance to the Creepy Caves.'

Bert patted Bob on the back so hard he nearly fell off the rug.

'Well, boys,' he said. 'It's goblin-bashing time.'

And the three trolls began to laugh, but Raven Boy didn't think they sounded as confident as they usually did, and his knees began to knock together at the thought of what might be to come.

Two

**Once Elf Girl found Rat
sleeping in one of her pointy
shoes, which made her so
cross she didn't speak for
a week.**

'We're too exposed up here!' said Raven Boy.

'Agreed,' said Elf Girl. 'Shona, find us
somewhere to land.'

Shona huffed, very huffily.

'Find us somewhere to land!' she cried.
'And do you just expect me to magic a hiding
place out of thin air? Look around! There's
nothing here!'

Elf Girl stared at her pointy boots, which

were definitely showing the miles they'd travelled.

'How about that?' said Raven Boy.

Elf Girl glanced up and saw what Raven Boy had seen: a small, ruined farmhouse, with no roof, and just four walls left standing.

'Better than nothing,' agreed Lord Socket. 'Carpet! Put us down there.'

Shona puffed herself up, ready to burst.

'My NAME is Shona and I don't like being given orders!'

'Shona,' said Raven Boy, soothingly, 'You're a very good carpet and it would be very nice if you could hide us inside that old building before some horrible monster controlled by the Goblin King comes and eats us for breakfast.'

Shona scowled at Socket, then huffed at Raven Boy, but she changed course and dropped neatly down inside the ruined farmhouse, just as the three trolls went through the painful and noisy process of turning back into men for the day.

'Ow!' said Bert.

'Ugh!' said Bob.

'Fooble-wooble!' said Cedric, and then there they were, three of the ugliest-looking

men you could lay eyes on.

Shona sighed.

'Thank goodness for that,' she said. 'You
lot are heavy. You know I'm still not sure I
should even carry eight passengers. Especially
since three of them are big fat hairy trolls!'

She glared at Bert, Bob and Cedric, who
looked hurt.

'Well,' said Bert, 'one of those eight is
just a tiny little rat so that evens us out, doesn't
it? Blooming cheeky rug!'

'Everyone's tired,' said Elf Girl. 'We've been flying all night. We can't go on till it's dark again so why don't we all just go to sleep?'

Raven Boy nodded.

'We'll be safe here,' he said, and they settled down, trying to find something comfortable to rest their heads on.

So they slept, which was good, although it turned out that Klingsor snored even worse than the trolls did.

They slept all morning, and through lunch, and it was finally about teatime when the first of them woke up, and that was Rat.

He woke because his tummy was telling him he'd missed at least two meals.

He nibbled Raven Boy's ear, trying to wake him, to see if he agreed that they ought to be eating something, but Raven Boy was sleeping so soundly that not even an ear-nibbling would wake him.

Feeling rather grumpy, Rat left Raven Boy to his dreams about squirrels and forests and decided to see if he could find any food.

He couldn't. The farmhouse was a

complete ruin. But Rat could see the windows of the old building and decided to have a look out to see what he could see, so he jumped up onto a windowsill.

He took one look outside, and was so shocked by what he saw that he immediately fell backwards onto Raven Boy's head.

Now Raven Boy woke up, and it was all Rat could do to squeak quickly and quietly before Raven Boy gave the game away.

'What's up?' whispered Raven Boy, and following Rat's twitching nose, Raven Boy peered over the windowsill too.

He sank back down again in hurry, and gulped.

'Eeep!' he said.

'EEEP, what?' asked Elf Girl, who was just waking up.

Raven Boy clamped his hand over her mouth, which Elf Girl didn't find very funny. She was starting to get pink ears when Raven Boy jabbed his finger towards the window.

Now Elf Girl saw what the other two had seen.

Around the house were creatures.

Lots of them.

They looked horrible. They looked like the meanest, foulest, most bad-tempered monstrosities ever. Some had dark red skin, some dark green, and some dark orange. They were covered in warts and had thin wisps of greasy hair. Long noses poked out over long chins and their ears were tall too. They wore armour made of leather and carried weapons of

all sorts: swords, bows, spears and axes.

'Goblins!' hissed Elf Girl.

Raven Boy nodded furiously, and
considered whether to faint first and scream
later, or the other way round, because outside
the farmhouse were not just one or two goblins,
or a few dozen, but thousands.

The friends were surrounded.

THREE

Trolls are well known for
being smelly, angry and rude.
But they are also very good at
flower arranging.

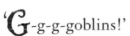

'**G**-g-g-goblins!'

Raven Boy clamped a hand over his own
mouth, as he and Elf Girl peered out at the
hordes outside.

'Oh my!' said Elf Girl, and her eyes
widened, as more and more and more goblins
seemed to be arriving all the time.

They watched in increasing terror, as
they realised what was going on.

'These are armies!' Raven Boy wailed, though he wailed quietly because the nearest goblins were not so far away from them. 'They're getting ready to go somewhere!'

'But they haven't seen us,' whispered Elf Girl. 'I don't think they know we're here.'

That much seemed to be true at least.

But then, a big red goblin in the nearest crowd cocked his head to one side. His eyes narrowed, and he turned towards the ruined farmhouse.

Raven Boy and Elf Girl slunk out of sight, breathing hard.

'He's coming this way!' '*E̲EEP!*' added Raven Boy. 'Quick, we have to get out of here! Wake the carpet up!'

Elf Girl crawled over to the rug and began to shake it.

'How do you wake a carpet up?' she muttered. 'Shona! Are you in there? It's time to wake up!'

'Hurry!' whispered Raven Boy.

'Has he seen us?'

'No,' said Raven Boy. 'But he's coming closer.'

'Shona!' cried Elf Girl. 'Please wake up!'

Then Klingsor sat bolt upright, shouting 'Eggs and bacon!' as he did so.

Raven Boy threw himself at the old magician, and stood on Cedric's foot, who howled so loudly that his two friends woke up shouting, 'Bash 'em! Bash 'em!' at the tops of their voices.

'Noo!' wailed Raven Boy, but at least the commotion had woken Shona, who was rubbing her eyes and looking like she'd just been dragged out of bed.

'What?' she snapped, grumpily.

'We have to go!' hissed Elf Girl. 'Now!' she added, as the big red goblin appeared at the window.

He stared in amazement, as if he couldn't understand what was going on, and then he roared a loud and terrible roar.

Just the smell of his breath was enough to turn Socket's hair from black to grey, and he jumped out of sleep, screaming at the sight of the goblin.

'Quick!' yelled Raven Boy to Elf Girl. 'Zap him with your bow!'

Elf Girl grabbed her bow, while Shona, who understood the danger they were in, flew a foot above the ground, and began to announce that they were leaving.

'Now!' she screamed, as Elf Girl fired her magic bow at the big red goblin. Elf Girl

was definitely getting better with her shooting:
this time she managed to turn the goblin into a
pretty white dog with a red bow in its
hair.

'Noooo!' wailed Raven
Boy.

'What?' shouted
Elf Girl. 'That worked!'

'I know, but now
there are a hundred and
fifty goblins all looking this
way. They're coming over!
Quick, Shona, get us out of
here.'

'Well, get on board
then!' cried Shona.

There was general
chaos and a certain amount of pandemonium as
the three trolls, in their human form, lumbered
onto the flying carpet. Klingsor was climbing
aboard when Elf Girl stepped backwards and
poked him in the eye with her bow.

'Your bow!' screamed Raven Boy, which
Shona misheard as 'Let's go!' and she shot into

the sky, straight out of the farmhouse ruin, with everyone just about aboard, although Socket was left clinging to the tassels at the rear end.

The trolls pulled him on board, and then they were speeding away, over what, they now saw, was a vast horde of goblins, stretching to the horizon in every direction.

'Oh golly,' said Raven Boy. 'There are millions of them.'

'Zillions,' said Elf Girl.

'How will we ever defeat them?' said Raven Boy.

'We can't!' said Elf Girl. 'That's it! We're doomed and so is the whole wide world.'

'We don't have to defeat them all,' said Klingsor, lying on his stomach. He rolled over and stood up.

'Please will passengers remember that—'

'Oh, Shona!' yelled Elf Girl. 'Put a sock in it! Klingsor, what did you just say?'

'I said, we don't have to defeat them all. Only one of them. You see, goblins are very mean and very nasty, but they are totally obedient to their master.'

'The Goblin King?'

'Exactly. So what we have to do is defeat the Goblin King, and then the rest of the goblins will just give up. And when I say "we",' Klingsor added, 'I do of course mean "you".'

And here, he pointed at Raven Boy.

'Oh, nuts,' said Raven Boy. 'I was afraid

you'd say that. I still have no idea how to defeat the Goblin King. This stupid Singing Sword has done nothing but wind everyone up, and the Tears of the Moon seem as magical as damp socks. And these goblins are enormous!'

He stared at the crowds of goblins, who were looking up, waving their weapons. One or two arrows flew at the carpet, but they were flying high enough to avoid them.

'So much for the element of surprise,' said Raven Boy. 'We were supposed to sneak unseen into the land of the Goblin King. And now look!'

It was a scary sight.

'I thought goblins were tiny,' said Raven Boy. 'That beast at the window was twice as tall as me!'

'You're thinking of pixies,' said Klingsor.

'Am I?' asked Raven Boy.

'You are,' said Klingsor.

'Listen!' Lord Socket said. 'That's all very well, but where are we going?'

'Good question,' said Elf Girl. 'But I'd say Shona already seems to know.'

Ahead, streaking towards them at top speed, were the Haunted Hills.

'Let's get on with this, shall we?' muttered Shona, and she made her landing announcement. 'Passengers will PLEASE take their seats for landing. Arrival at the Creepy Caves in ten minutes. I repeat, arrival—'

'Yes!' interrupted Raven Boy. 'We heard the first time.'

Now, there was nothing for it; it was time to enter the land of the Goblin King.

FOUR

The thing about trolls and flower arranging? That wasn't actually true.

'Look!' moaned Raven Boy. 'They're following us!'

He was right. Vast numbers of goblins were leaving the plains and were now running after the flying carpet, shrieking and howling. The only good news was that Shona the flying rug was fast, very fast in fact, and sped away from the pursuing hordes.

'We need to lose them!' cried Elf Girl. 'Get out of sight.'

'But how?' Lord Socket yelled, pulling himself a bit further away from the edge of the carpet. 'These Haunted Hills are empty and bare – there's nowhere to hide at all.'

That was true, but no one had time to say anything more, because a great burst of flame shot down from the sky, just missing the carpet.

'EEEP!' cheeped Raven Boy. He rolled onto his back and then screamed as a huge fire-breathing dragon came flapping towards them.

'Sho-na!' Elf Girl screeched.

'I've seen it!' Shona snapped, and she flew even faster than she was flying before, as another bolt of flame whizzed past them, singeing the tassels on the back of the rug.

'Ow!' screeched Shona.

Raven Boy shook Elf Girl by her shoulders.

'Quick! Elf Girl! Do something!'

Elf Girl was shaking so badly she could barely hold her bow as the dragon wheeled around for a third strike.

Elf Girl fired, and a flock of pigeons sprang from her bow and hurtled towards the

dragon, who opened his mouth and gobbled them in one gulp.

'I can't concentrate!' Elf Girl said. 'I'm too scared.'

'Try again!' shouted Socket, waving his hands above his head in panic, but the dragon was already coming back for another try at turning them into a giant flying piece of toast.

'There!' cried Raven Boy. 'Shona! That wood!'

Raven Boy had seen that tucked into one of the valleys of the Haunted Hills was a rather scrappy forest. It looked small and poky from up in the air, but it might just be enough to save them.

Shona lurched and tilted towards the trees, flying so steeply that her eight passengers tumbled forwards and had to struggle to stay on board.

'Eeeeeeee!' they yelled, at the tops of their voices, and the dragon changed direction and hurtled after them, sucking in a huge breath, ready to send a scorching blast of fire.

But Shona was fast, and zipped into the woodland, darting between the trees. The dragon, being that much larger, saw way too late that it was about to hit the trees, and there was a splintering crash as it ploughed into the forest.

Shona zigged and zagged and was so scared that she wouldn't slow down, even though Raven Boy was shouting at her to stop.

Finally, the message got through that the dragon was gone, and she slowed down, cruising through the woodland, which, now that they were inside, was much bigger than Raven Boy had thought.

'I thought I liked forests,' Raven Boy said. 'But this place is creepy.'

Elf Girl nodded.

'It's even scarier than Fright Forest,' she agreed.

It was dark and dank and they could sense that nasty things were lurking in the undergrowth, out of sight, but watching them.

'Could someone check my tassels?' Shona said. 'I feel like they're on fire.'

Socket, who was closest, had a look.

'You are smouldering,' he announced. 'Allow me.'

With that, he pulled a bottle of water from out of his coat and sprinkled a little on her fringe.

'Oooh,' said Shona, 'Thank you. That

feels so much better.'

'Well now,' said Klingsor. 'How are things going? Very well, yes?'

Everyone stared at him as if he was mad, which, to be fair, he probably was. Bob was about to push him off the rug and was only stopped by Bert and Cedric.

'Come along!' said Klingsor. 'Things are going rather well, aren't they? Here we are, in the Haunted Hills, all alive, no one eaten, stabbed or burnt.'

'Yet,' said Elf Girl.

Klingsor ignored her.

'So now what we need to do is find the entrance to the Creepy Caves.'

'Which could be anywhere!' Raven Boy sighed.

'Indeed!' said Klingsor. 'Which is why we need to try using magic. If the carpet could stop for a short time, I can perform a small magical spell which will show us the way to the caves.'

'You can?'

'I can.'

Klingsor set to work. From the folds of his cloak he pulled a bag, and from the bag he pulled some smaller bags, and from the smaller bags he pulled some herbs, which he sprinkled on the carpet.

'I hope you're going to clean that up,' said Shona, grumpily.

'Shh!' said Raven Boy. 'He's doing magic.'

It didn't look like magic. It looked like Klingsor was staring at a mess of dried herbs on a carpet, but suddenly he stuck his head up, thrust a hand out, and declared, 'That way!'

So that was the way they went.

FIVE

**Klingsor the magician is a
very old wizard indeed, and
has used his magical powers
to live longer than normal,
much longer.**

Shona flew steadily in the direction that
Klingsor told her to.

They were all exhausted from the flight
from the goblins and the dragon, and lay
around on the carpet (rather untidily, in Shona's
opinion). Even the big and fearless trolls seemed
to have been scared into silence by their close
encounter with the dragon.

'Is it far?' Raven Boy asked Klingsor,

from time to time, but all the old magician would answer was, 'Not far, not far.'

Elf Girl sat by Raven Boy, staring at the trees and looking thoughtful.

'Raven Boy?' she said.

'Yes, Elf Girl?'

'You remember how all this started?'

Raven Boy nodded.

'I fell through the trees and landed on your hut.'

'And squashed it flat.'

'It was the tree I was falling in that squashed it. Not me.'

'True,' said Elf Girl. 'Then we were nearly eaten by that big ogre.'

'No,' said Raven Boy.

'No?'

'No. First you decided to call me Raven Boy.'

'Oh yes!' said Elf Girl. 'That's right. And I still don't know your real name. Why won't you tell me?'

'Because I'm really embarrassed by it.'

'I'm embarrassed by mine, but you know that.'

'Yes, E—'

Elf Girl stuck her fist inside Raven Boy's mouth.

'Don't ever say it!' she said, 'especially when there's other people about.'

'Mm-mmm,' said Raven Boy, nodding and holding up his hands.

Elf Girl took her fist out of his mouth.

'Make me a promise,' Elf Girl said.

'What?'

'If we get out of this alive, and defeat the Goblin King, then you'll tell me your real name.'

Raven Boy thought about this.

'Maybe,' he said, but he was smiling.

'Rolo!' said Elf Girl, suddenly, but Raven Boy shook his head, laughing.

'Not even close,' he said, and they drifted on through the dark forest.

'But it begins with an R?'

'You know it does.'

'Rudolph!'

'You tried that when we first met. It wasn't right then and it isn't right now.'

Elf Girl sulked for a moment or two, and then cried, 'Ricky!'

'Forget it,' said Raven Boy. 'You really will never guess.'

Despite the fact that she would never guess, Elf Girl was about to have another try when the whole forest around them seemed to sneeze.

The trees shuddered and shivered. The nine adventurers stared at the leaves, waiting for something to happen, and then it did.

All at once, from nowhere, vicious-looking monkeys swung out at them and began to scratch, bite, pick and chew at everything and anything.

'Ow!' screeched Raven Boy.

'Talk to them!' squealed Elf Girl. 'Tell them to stop!'

'Do they look like they're in the mood for a conversation?' shouted Raven Boy, pulling a monkey off his face and chucking him off the side of the rug.

'Shona!'

'I know!' snapped Shona, and once again she found herself speeding away from trouble. The monkeys didn't give up, however, and even as Bob and Bert bashed the last of them on the head and sent them spinning over the side, more monkeys swung out of the treetops.

'Faster!' yelled Lord Socket.

'I can't!' moaned Shona. 'I'm tired.'

'Nonsense! Rugs don't get tired.'

'This one does,' said Shona, but she did her best to speed up, whipping between the trees at such high speed that the monkeys started to lag behind.

Raven Boy stood up, and thumbed his nose at the last of the monkeys.

'Er, I say, carpet . . .' began Klingsor, but no one was listening to him. Which was a shame, because if they had, they would have heard what he was trying to say.

'Miss Carpet, I think we ought to stop now . . .'

It was no use. Everyone else, even Shona, had joined Raven Boy in jumping up and down and waving bye-bye to the monkeys.

Then, Cedric jumped a little higher and was whacked on the head by a branch. He went flying and grabbed out, managing to pull Bert and Bob off the carpet with him.

'Oh!' said Raven Boy, who was leaning

over the side to see where they'd fallen. There was no sign of the trolls, but just a big hole between the trees.

And then, Shona flew slap bang into a tree.

They tumbled up into the air, and then they tumbled down, and Raven Boy was waiting for a thump as he hit the ground but, to his surprise, it didn't come.

Everything had gone black. He could hear Elf Girl wailing, and he could hear the Singing Sword too, because he'd let go of it as he fell.

'You're the one for me,' it sang, but just as it was getting into its stride, they hit the ground.

'Ow!' said Raven Boy.

'Uff!' cried Elf Girl.

'You're as lovely as a tree,' sang the Singing Sword.

Raven Boy scrabbled around and found the sword, to stop it singing any more.

'Where are we?' said Elf Girl.

It was dark, but Raven Boy could make out the glow of Elf Girl's bowstring. She was holding it ready to shoot.

'Good idea,' Raven Boy said, and looked around.

They were alone.

They were alone in a set of caves, and the caves were, to put it mildly, a little bit creepy.

'Where are we?' repeated Elf Girl.

'I'll give you one guess,' said Raven Boy.

'The Creepy Caves?' said Elf Girl.

'That was too easy, wasn't it?' said Raven Boy, who decided it was a good time to faint, so he did.

'As lovely as a tree,
you're the one for me,'

sang the sword.

Elf Girl stamped her foot.

'Raven Boy, wake up now or I'll kill you!'

But Raven Boy was out cold, and so Elf Girl was left with the sword for company, who had a happy little song to sing about bunny rabbits in love.

Six

**When Raven Boy was little,
he used to actually think he
was a bird. Fortunately he
never tried to fly off anything
too high before he realised
he wasn't.**

It wasn't only Raven Boy and Elf Girl who
were alone in the dark. All nine of the companions
had tumbled down through holes in the forest
floor and were now not only lost, but separated
too.

Lord Socket had been the last to fall and,
as he'd done so, he'd grabbed hold of Shona's
tassels, pulling her with him.

Startled, she'd tried to fly back up the

hole, but a load of old logs and other rubbish from the forest had pelted after them, and trapped them in some kind of tunnel.

'That wasn't very clever,' said Shona.

'I had little choice,' said Socket, rather sniffily. 'Where are we, anyway?'

'I'll give you one guess,' said Shona.

'The Creepy Caves?'

'That was easy,' said Shona.

'Who said it had to be hard? Anyway, what next? It's awfully gloomy down here.'

Shona huffed and puffed and a moment or two later, two small beams of light shone from the front of the carpet.

'Headlights?' exclaimed Socket. 'I didn't know flying carpets had headlights.'

'It seems you don't know very much at all,' muttered Shona. 'You lordly types. Stuck up in that castle of yours with someone waiting on you hand and foot. The Sultan was just the same.'

'The Sultan?' asked Socket, wondering what he'd ever done to offend the flying rug.

'The man who owned me until I was captured by Elf Girl and Raven Boy.'

'They captured you? They don't seem
like the sort of people to kidnap a carpet.'

'Well, as it happens, they're not so bad,'
Shona said. 'But if you ever tell them I said that,
I'll tip you down a volcano.'

Socket held his hands up.

'All right, all right,' he said. 'Gosh, you
are quite uptight, aren't you?'

'Uptight?' screamed Shona. 'You'd be

57

uptight if you were in my position.' At this point, she humphed so loudly that Socket thought she was about to explode. 'Get on!' she said grumpily. 'We need to get out of here before something nasty comes and gets us.'

'Agreed,' said Socket, and climbed back onto the carpet. 'Which way?' he added.

'Who knows?' asked Shona.

They looked ahead of them and they looked behind them and both directions looked equally frightening.

'We may as well go forwards,' said Shona, and she set off.

As they flew, Socket sat on the carpet, thinking.

'Shona?' he said.

'What?'

'Now please don't get all shouty again, but . . . I

wonder if you could tell me exactly what you meant earlier? What position are you in?'

'Isn't it obvious?' Shona grumped.

'Well, no, not really. In fact.'

Shona sighed.

'I don't like being a carpet. Is that clear enough for you?'

Socket scratched his head.

'But haven't you always been a carpet?'

'Of course I haven't!' squealed Shona.

'Shh!' hushed Socket. 'Something might hear you!'

Shona shivered as she knew that the snooty young lord was probably right.

'Of course I haven't always been a carpet,' she whispered. 'Once upon a time I was a normal girl like anyone else. Then the Sultan's wizard turned me into the pilot of this carpet. That was years ago and I hate it!'

'Oh!' said Socket. 'That's awful. And that's why you're grumpy all the time?'

'I am not grumpy!' screamed Shona, which made Socket wince in fear of being discovered by goblins.

'No!' he said, hurriedly. 'Of course you're not. I can see that now. Well, that's terrible. Ooh. That tickles.'

'What tickles?' asked Shona, confused.

'You just tickled me with your tassels,' said Socket.

'I did not!' cried Shona.

'Well, something . . . Ooh! There it is again.'

Lord Socket stroked something from his face.

'There's . . . Ugh! Something hanging from the ceiling.'

'Cobwebs!' said Shona. 'I am never going to get myself clean, am I?'

By the weak headlights of the carpet they could see cobwebs stretching across the tunnel. They were getting thicker.

'Maybe we should turn back?' suggested Socket.

'Good idea,' agreed Shona, but when she turned round, they saw something that told them it was a very bad idea, because coming down the tunnel behind them were lights. Burning torchlight, heading their way.

'Only one thing for it!' Shona cried. 'Fly through the cobwebs, if we can. Hold on!'

She charged into the spiders' webs, which were getting thicker than ever. At first, she managed to break through the sticky stuff, but as they flew, she got caught in larger and stronger webs until, finally, with a great groan, they ground to a halt.

Socket glanced behind them, and saw that the torchlight was getting nearer and nearer. And then Shona the carpet let out an almighty scream as she peered into the dark ahead.

There, looming out of the gloom, was an enormous spider, almost as wide as the tunnel itself, its eight legs skipping through the webs with ease. It shot out great sticky strands and in a moment they were spun into a ball of goo, stuck fast so tight they couldn't even scream.

Just then, around the corner came the source of the torchlights: a group of nasty smelly goblins, looking for trouble.

'Heh, heh, heh,' said the one in charge. 'Look what we got!'

They started to edge closer.

Seven

**Goblins smell even worse
than trolls, and it's mostly
because of what they eat, and
how they eat it. Plus they
never brush their teeth.**

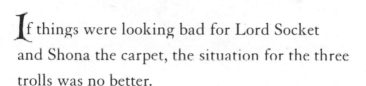

If things were looking bad for Lord Socket
and Shona the carpet, the situation for the three
trolls was no better.

They hurtled down their hole for what
seemed like forever. They'd fallen so far that
the drop ought to have squashed them flat but,
luckily, they landed on something soft.

Unluckily, the soft thing was an underground river, and they were swept away by it,

charging off into a dark tunnel.

'Help!' spluttered Cedric as soon as he got his head out of the water for long enough. 'I can't swim!'

'Neither can I!' wailed Bob.

'Nor me!' screeched Bert. 'We're doomed!'

That was about all they had time to say before they went underwater again, tumbling about in the raging river like leaves in the wind.

On and on they went, as the river turned and twisted down steep chutes and around long curves, and then, at last, they felt themselves falling, and from the sound around them, they could tell they were falling into somewhere bigger than the tunnel. Much, much bigger, in fact

They'd shot out over a waterfall, which poured the river into a vast underground lake.

'Eeeeee!' wailed Cedric as they fell.

'Oooooh!' cried Bob.

And, 'Ulp!' gulped Bert, gasping for air.

Then, with an almighty splosh, they hit the surface of the lake, and went underwater again.

When they came up, spluttering and coughing and batting at the water with their big clumsy fists, they were very bedraggled trolls indeed.

'I still can't swim!' said Cedric, choking.

'Nah, really?' Bert managed to cough, before going under once more.

'Do something!' squealed Bob, sounding like a little girl, as he bobbed up for a moment, but there was nothing they could do.

Then, something happened.

One minute they were bobbing about in the water, and the next there was a whooshing, and they were all three gobbled up by a vast mouth attached to the business end of a sea monster.

'Oh,' said Cedric.

'What is it?' asked Bob.

'You two are such numpties!' wailed Bert. 'We've been eaten, of course!'

'Eaten?' asked Cedric.

'Eaten?' asked Bob.

'Yes!' screamed Bert. 'Eaten!'

'Well,' said Cedric. 'I don't like that. We're supposed to be the ones doing the eating, aren't we?'

'Yeah,' said Bob. 'Not the other way round. I feel . . .'

He searched for the right word.

'Funny?' asked Bert.

'Nah,' said Bob. 'I feel . . .'

'Silly?' suggested Cedric.

'Nah,' said Bob. 'I feel . . .'

'What?' cried Bert.

'Angry!' said Bob. 'I feel angry!'

'Yeah, me too,' said Cedric.

Bert chuckled. It was an evil chuckle.

'Yeah,' he said. 'Me three. Right. So what are we gonna do about it?'

In the lake, the sea monster was swimming along feeling very pleased with itself for having had enough food to count as breakfast, lunch and an afternoon snack all at once. Then, it felt something strange. It was coming from inside. From inside its belly.

Suddenly, it had the most terrible tummy ache it had ever had, as it seemed that the food it had eaten was fighting back.

'Ow!' said the sea monster to itself, as, deep inside, the three trolls were punching and kicking and even chewing their way out.

The monster swam on a bit more.

'Garp!' it went.

Then, 'Bulp!'

And then, finally, 'Ga-roomp!' and it stuck its head out of the water and let rip with the loudest burp of all time.

The three trolls flew out of the monster's mouth and through the air, end over end, screaming as they went, though Cedric was still chewing on a bit of sea monster stomach.

Then, with three great thumps, the trolls landed on a beach at the far side of the lake, just in time to see the sea monster slink away underwater, feeling very sorry for itself.

'That showed 'im,' said Cedric, still chewing.

'Don't speak with your mouth full,' said Bert.

'Why not?' asked Bob. 'We're trolls. We're supposed to be unpleasant.'

Bert thought about that.

'Good point,' said Bert. ''Ere, 'ave you noticed sumfin'?'

'What's that?' said Cedric.

'We can see!' said Bert. 'We're underground, but it's not dark.'

They looked up and saw that the roof of the gigantic cavern was glowing slightly, casting a weak light on everything. The lake stretched away before them, the water calm again now that the sea monster had gone off to sulk.

'Now what?' asked Bob.

'We get what we came for,' said Bert.

'What did we come for?' asked Cedric.

'You know!' said Bert. 'We want what the Goblin King got, don't we? You remember, doncha?'

'Oh,' said Cedric. 'No.'

Bert slapped his forehead with his big fat fist.

'You are the stupidest troll I ever . . .'

'Well,' said Cedric. 'What's wrong with that? We're supposed to be stupid, aren't we?'

Bert thought about that too.

'Yeah,' he said. 'Good point. Anyway, you remember why we came? To get the thing the Goblin King's got?'

'I remember!' said Bob, suddenly. 'The mys-tic-al thingy of wotsit.'

Bert sighed.

'The mystical ring of power,'

he said. 'And then we won't have to keep changing into trolls every night! Right?'

'Right!' said the other two.

'Hey!' said Bob. 'Look! There's a tunnel!'

There was indeed a tiny tunnel leading off the beach. With no other option but to try and swim for it again, it seemed clear that that was the way they had to go.

Then, without warning, from out of the tunnel entrance, poured goblins. Lots of goblins. Thousands of them, in fact.

Bert gulped.

Bob gulped.

And Cedric muttered.

'Right, lads. It's goblin-bashing time.'

EIGHT

Goblins not only smell, they
are extremely dim-witted and
very cross most of the time.
But they are very good at
flower arranging.

While Socket and Shona were wrestling with
a spider and the trolls were doing their best
to knock a thousand goblins into the lake,
Klingsor and Rat had fallen down a third hole,
much shorter than the others, and landed with a
slight bump on a rough cave floor.

'Squeak!' said Rat.

'Well I never!' said Klingsor.

A little light shone down from the hole

down which they'd fallen, and it showed them two things.

First, that there was no way that Klingsor would be able to climb back up the hole, even if Rat might have been able to. And, second, it showed them that they were sitting in a cave from which at least six tunnels led off.

'Squeak,' said Rat. He didn't sound too sure about his squeak, though, something which Klingsor hadn't failed to notice.

'Yes,' he said. 'Quite a conundrum, eh?'

Rat squeaked.

'A conundrum. A puzzle,' said Klingsor. 'Hard to know which way to go.'

Klingsor stood up and stared into each of the tunnels in turn, but they all looked the same.

'Do you have any ideas, my furry friend?' asked Klingsor, and Rat squeaked.

'I wish I could understand you like the feathery boy can,' said Klinsgor, but he shrugged. 'But maybe you understand me. We need to find the others. We're no use all split up! We have to be nine to defeat the Goblin King, because nine is a magic number. Whereas two is just . . . well. Two is just us, isn't it?'

Rat squeaked.

'Do you know which way to go?' asked Klingsor, peering closely at Rat.

Rat squeaked about fifteen times in a row, and then set off down one of the tunnels at great speed.

'Hey!' cried Klingsor. 'Not so fast! Wait for me! I'm an old wizard, you know, and you have twice as many legs as me!'

Rat had disappeared down the tunnel,
and as Klingsor followed, he rummaged in his
cloak and pulled out a small jewel which, when
he whispered some magic words, started to
glow with a pale green light.

'There we are!' he said happily. 'Now,
where's that small rodent got to? Bless me, but
he's a speedy critter.'

And so Klingsor went on muttering to himself as he made his way along the tunnel. He knew he couldn't have lost Rat yet because there had been no other passages leading off this tunnel, but he would have been happier if he'd been able to see his small furry companion.

As he went, it started to get warm in the tunnel, even though it had been very cold in the first cave.

Klingsor was wearing his large cloak, but there was no time to think about taking it off, despite the fact that the tunnel was getting very warm indeed. Almost hot, in fact.

The old wizard whispered a few more magic words to the jewel and it shone more brightly, and there, at the turn of the tunnel, he saw Rat, at last.

'There you are!' declared Klingsor.

Rat squeaked.

He sounded very excited. In fact, he was so excited that he was jumping up and down, and when he saw Klingsor coming, he ran towards him and then bounced around in front of him for a bit.

'Found something, have you?' asked Klingsor. 'One of our friends? Who is it? Lord Socket, perhaps? Or the smelly trolls?'

Rat bounded away from Klingsor once more, turned out of sight around the corner, and it was all the old man could do to hobble after him.

It was hotter than ever as Klingsor emerged from the tunnel into the new cave that Rat had found.

There was no one there. What there was, instead, was what looked very much like a kitchen, though it was a strange and scary place.

Suspended on long chains attached to the ceiling, vast cooking pots hung over open fires that roared like the furnaces of hell. Along the walls of the cave were alcoves and shelves stuffed with jars full of strange foods, and there were big pots on the floor that held cooking equipment that looked more like it belonged in a torture chamber than a kitchen.

Rat was happily sniffing his way along a shelf, trying to get into some of the jars.

'Oh you silly thing!' declared Klingsor.

'Thinking with your stomach! We were supposed to be finding our friends!'

Rat squeaked in a sort of way which meant that he'd be happier looking for people if he wasn't so hungry, and Klingsor shuffled over to him to see what he had found.

'What's this then?' Klingsor said, peering at the label on a large jar of something green and sludgy, but the label was written in Goblin, and Klingsor couldn't read it.

'Come on,' said the old wizard to Rat. 'I really don't think this is safe. We ought to get out of here right this minute, before someone comes back. There are things cooking in those pots; they won't be gone long.'

Rat squeaked, in the sort of way that meant he was going to eat before they left and he wasn't going to argue about it. He turned to squeak at Klingsor again, and then he saw something which made the hairs on his back stand up on end and his whiskers curl up tight.

Klingsor had a very bad feeling.

He turned slowly, and there was a goblin; only one, but one very large goblin, with an apron

round his waist and a very large metal spoon in
his hand.

    'Oh,' said Klingsor. 'Oh dear.'

NINE

**That thing about goblins
and flower arranging?
It's not strictly true.**

While all these things were going on, Elf Girl
was waiting for Raven Boy to come round from
his latest fainting fit. She was starting to doubt
that Raven Boy was the 'chosen one', the wise
fool that Klingsor had spoken about, and she
was also seriously starting to doubt whether they
would ever be able to defeat the Goblin King.

Her one success was that she'd found
that the sword would stop singing if she just

put Raven Boy's hand on it, even though he was out cold. That made her feel better, because the sword had a knack of getting on everybody's nerves. Everybody except Rat, who danced about with a dreamy look on his face as soon as the sword got a chance to sing.

Finally Raven Boy sat up, rubbing his head.

'I think we fell down a hole,' he said. 'I think we're in the Creepy Caves.'

'Is that right?' asked Elf Girl. 'Raven Boy, you are amazing.'

'I am?'

'You are. Amazingly stupid.'

'Well, there's no need to be rude,' said Raven Boy.

'Isn't there?' asked Elf Girl. 'I've been sitting in this dark tunnel for half an hour while you were snoring, and anything could have come and got us right then and there and you'd have known nothing about it! So I think I have every right to be rude!'

Raven Boy stood up while Elf Girl finished ranting at him. 'I'm sorry,' he said. 'It's just all a bit much. This whole thing. We'll never do it!'

Elf Girl nodded sadly.

'I was thinking the same thing,' she said,
and then she added, 'And I'm sorry too.'

They smiled at each other.

'We have to find some way out of here,'
said Elf Girl. 'Because I can't keep pulling on my
bowstring and making light forever, you know.'

'Oh!' said Raven Boy. 'Of course not.
Come on. Let's try this way. We need to find the
others.'

They set off along the tunnel, which looked very much the same in either direction. After they had been stomping along for some time, Raven Boy grabbed Elf Girl's elbow.

'What?' she asked, but Raven Boy put his finger to her lips.

'Shh! Something's coming.'

'I can't hear anything.'

'I can,' said Raven Boy desperately. 'Quick! In here!'

He pulled Elf Girl into a little alcove in the rough wall of the tunnel. Soon, she realised that Raven Boy was right. There was the sound of marching feet, and then, down the tunnel, came goblins. Hundreds of them, marching in time.

'More soldiers for the Goblin army!' whispered Elf Girl. 'Oh, Raven Boy. How will we ever defeat them all?'

Raven Boy shook his head, and watched in terror as goblin after goblin marched past.

Finally, they disappeared down the tunnel and when Elf Girl came out again, she saw that she didn't need to light her bowstring, because ahead of them was a weird red glow.

They emerged into a huge cavern and soon found the source of the light. Enormous stalactites hung from the ceiling, and stalagmites just as big pushed their way up to join their cousins. Winding its way across the middle was the source of the light – a river of molten lava, so hot that it glowed red and even white in places. It cast an eerie flickering light around the cave and was very, very spooky indeed.

'EEP,' said Raven Boy. 'Look!'

He pointed at the remains of a bridge across the river. At some point, it must have collapsed, leaving no way across the molten rock.

'Well, that's that,' said Elf Girl. 'We'll have to go back the way we came.'

They turned and were about to set off when they heard the sound of more feet, and then, out of the tunnel, came a horde of horrible goblins.

They took one look at Raven Boy and Elf Girl, and then began screaming and running towards them.

'Run!' wailed Raven Boy.

'Where?' panted Elf Girl as she ran. 'There's nowhere to go.'

'There!' cried Raven Boy, pointing at the molten river.

'What?' screeched Elf Girl, as she saw what Raven Boy was thinking.

There were solid rocks floating in the river of lava, like little moving islands. If they timed it right, they could hop across them like stepping-stones and make it to the far side.

'No!' yelled Elf Girl, but it was too late, Raven Boy was already leaping through the air.

He wobbled a little, but made it to the nearest rock, landing on all fours. He turned.

'Come on!'

And Elf Girl jumped and landed next to him. The goblins howled in anger as Raven Boy and Elf Girl made the next jump to a bigger rock in the middle of the river.

The goblins howled even louder.

Or so it seemed, but then Elf Girl noticed something.

'They're laughing!' she said. 'Why are they laughing?'

Elf Girl glanced at the far side of the
river, and saw what the goblins had seen. And
that was more goblins, blocking their escape.

Raven Boy and Elf Girl stood completely
still as the rock drifted downstream. They were
heading for a low tunnel.

'We can't,' said Elf Girl, and then she
screamed, because the rock they were standing on
split into two, with her on one half, and Raven
Boy on the other.

Before they had time to think, their two
floating rocks disappeared into the tunnel of
molten lava, with the sound of howling goblins
ringing in their ears.

TEN

If there's one thing that Rat
loves doing most, it's eating.
His main complaint about
the whole 'saving the world'
business is there's never
enough time for eating.

ElfGirl scooted along wondering how she'd
ever got into such a mess. Life was very simple
when she lived in Fright Forest with her family and
friends nearby. But ever since the hut squashing
had started, it seemed that her life had been in
constant danger.

She felt very cross and her ears went as
red as the molten lava, and then she felt even
crosser when she realised there was no one to be

angry with.

On and
on she went,
bobbing about on
her solid piece
of rock, when
suddenly the
tunnel emerged
into a bigger cave
again.

There was
a shore not so far
away, but too far
away for her to
jump. Then she had
a brilliant idea. She'd made her bow do all sorts
of strange magic when she was learning to use
it; in fact, one of the first things she'd done was
to trap the trolls in a block of ice. If she could
manage to freeze the lava, she would be able to
walk across it to safety.

She didn't have long; there was another
tunnel ahead of her, and so she began to fire
away at the molten rock, but she was feeling

very panicky, and nothing seemed to work.
She fired a stream of strange items at the lava,
such as umbrellas, followed by a hen (which
managed to fly away before becoming a roast
chicken), and after that she let loose a barrel of
apples, four rainbows and finally a grandfather
clock.

The clock hit the far bank, then toppled backwards towards her, but the end of it landed on her rock, making a little bridge to the bank.

It was wobbly, but there was no time left, so she skipped across to the shore, just in time to see the clock topple into the molten lava and be instantly vaporised.

'Phew!' she said, and looked around.

She was in another creepy cave, with stalactites and stalagmites around her, forming weird shapes that were like the faces of monsters.

One of them was particularly realistic. It looked just like the face of a huge rock monster, and Elf Girl had to look at it twice to be sure that it wasn't the real thing. When she looked at it a third time, however, she could have sworn that it had moved, and then, when she looked at it for a fourth time, she saw its eyes open, and its horrible big mouth open too, gnashing its teeth.

'Where's bird boy when you need him?' wailed Elf Girl. 'Eep!'

The rock monster lumbered to its feet and started to shuffle towards Elf Girl.

She pulled her bow into shape once

more, and for once, fired exactly what she
wanted to; a string of really sharp arrows, but as
they hit the monster, they pinged off, snapping
like dry twigs on his stone body.

'Oh no!' Elf Girl shrieked.

She tried again, backing away as the rock monster came closer to her, and fired a pillow full of feathers.

The monster sneezed a couple of times, but was otherwise unhurt. It stumbled towards Elf Girl, who saw that she only had one chance left.

This time, she concentrated really hard, and out of the bow came a blinding beam of light, so bright that she had to shut her eyes.

When she opened them again, there was nothing in front of her. The monster had gone, and all she could see was a trail of molten rock trickling away.

'Yay!' she shouted. 'Raven Boy! I did it!'

Then she stopped shouting, and felt very lonely indeed, as she remembered that Raven Boy, and everyone else, was a long way away from her.

'Come on,' she said to herself. 'This won't do. I have to keep walking and I'll find the others.'

She set off again, looking for a way out, and just when she was starting to think there wasn't one, she found a tiny tunnel that even she could barely stand upright in. She stooped and headed into the darkness once more, pulling her bowstring so that it glowed.

Up and up she went, around tight corners and along twisting passages. The tunnel seemed the same all the way along, the same rough grey rock, and she was beginning to wonder if she would ever get out again, when she tripped over something on the rough floor and went sprawling.

She dropped her bow, and so was surprised that there was still light when she opened her eyes.

She was even more surprised to see, right in front of her nose, a very large and hairy pair of feet, bright orange in colour, with horrible long toenails that really needed cutting.

She lifted her head, and found herself staring up into the face of the ugliest goblin she could imagine. He was looking at her with a wicked smile on his face, holding a burning torch in one hand and a large sack in the other.

'Just wait till the King sees you!' he snarled and, before Elf Girl could move, she found herself inside the sack.

ELEVEN

Elf Girl thinks Raven Boy might have grown an inch or two since they first met in the forest. Either that or she's shrinking.

I f things were bad for Elf Girl, Raven Boy wasn't doing much better.

'E**EP!**' he cried, as he disappeared down a different tunnel. 'Elf Girl! Come back!'

There was no more chance of that than of the river freezing over, and soon Raven Boy was alone, bobbing about on the rock. The stream of lava he was on started to get faster, and rougher, and he had to balance with his arms to stay on.

Then, Raven Boy realised that something even worse was happening; the rock on which he was standing was cracking up. Small pieces were breaking off, and the piece he was on was getting smaller and smaller and smaller. Very soon, there'd be nothing left at all, and then he wouldn't even have a chance to be melted, but would be instantly destroyed in a flash of feathery flame.

'Eeeeeep!' he cried, as the rock split into two, right down the middle, with one foot on each piece.

They started to drift apart and Raven
Boy hopped onto the larger one, but even that
was still breaking up.

He looked around frantically. The walls of
the tunnel were rough, rough enough, he reckoned,
to climb on. It would mean leaping from his floating
rock to get to the wall, but he had no choice.

Raven Boy leapt, and thanks to his amazing
tree-climbing skills, he found himself clinging to
the rock wall.

'I would really like to faint right now,'
he announced, to no one in particular, but he
knew he couldn't.

Slowly, he made his way along the wall,
which, since he was so good at climbing, was
quite easy.

The only problem was that there didn't
seem to be anywhere to go. On and on the tunnel
went, and it was hot. The molten lava was making
him sweat like a pig in an overcoat, and that made
his hands slippery.

Eventually, he saw the tunnel widening,
and the roof lifted, and then he was in a vast
cavern, quite the largest one that he'd seen so far.

The ceiling soared
up; the far side was so far
away that it couldn't be
seen, and it was full of the
craziest stone formations
that you could imagine.

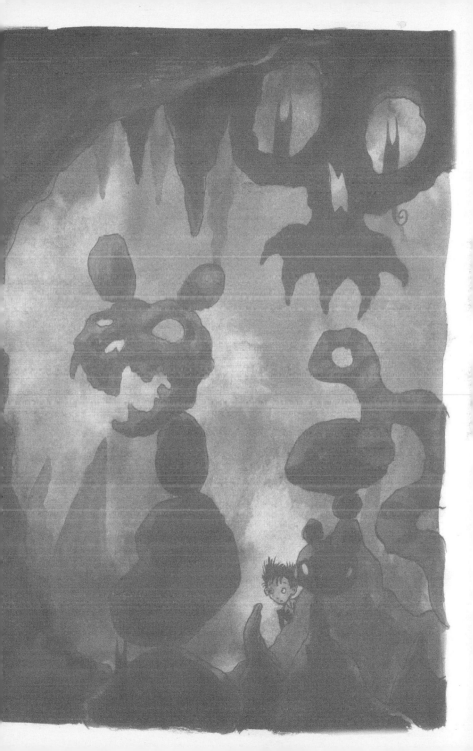

And it was illuminated once more by the red glow of the molten river of rock.

Raven Boy sidled down from the rock wall of the river and hopped to safety on the floor.

From somewhere in the distance, he could hear noises. There was more light too, flickering somewhere ahead.

He decided there was nothing else to do but to creep forward and see what was going on. Slowly and as quietly as only a Raven Boy can be, he snuck this way and that. The glow was getting brighter, and the noise getting louder.

He could hear chanting. There were shouts, loud and vicious cries that chilled him to the bone. He turned a corner and now he could see terrible shadows flung onto the walls of the cave. They were shadows he didn't want to see; of goblins dancing about, waving spears and swords.

Raven Boy shivered again. Whoever controlled these terrifying creatures must be all-powerful and super-strong; the most awful of them all, the Goblin King. Raven Boy knew there was no way he would be able to defeat him, even if they knew what to do with the

Singing Sword and the Tears of the Moon.
Thinking about the tears made him think of Elf
Girl. He hoped she had them safe. Then he just
hoped that Elf Girl was safe.

He stuck his head around another corner,
and wished he hadn't.

It seemed he had walked right into the
centre of all the goblin fun. A thousand pairs of
goblin eyes were turned towards him.

'EEP,' he said, in a tiny, tiny voice, and
before he could do anything else he was lifted
off the floor by two strong goblins, and carried
into the centre of the hall.

Then he saw his friends.

They were suspended in wooden cages
above an even larger river of molten lava.

There was Klingsor, with Rat peeping
out from his cloak.

In another cage was Socket.

In three separate cages were the trolls,
who waved at him, calling, 'Coo-ee!' and 'Ahoy,
Bird Boy!'

And in the final cage was Elf Girl, without
her bow, looking sad and scared at the same time.

On the ground nearby were a couple of things: a rolled-up rug, and a bottle of water.

'Oh, no,' she said. 'Not you too!'

Raven Boy shrugged.

'Yup,' he said. 'Me too.'

Suddenly, the noisy goblins were silent. It was eerie how, in that vast place, so many goblins could be so still, and then the friends knew why. The whisper was going around the hall – the Goblin King was coming!

Raven Boy felt the sword snatched from his hand, which immediately began to sing a cheesy love song, and then, along one of the walls, Raven Boy saw the huge shadow of the Goblin King approaching.

The goblins fell to their knees, bowing their heads, and then, there he was.

The Goblin King. He marched straight to Raven Boy, and Raven Boy was so scared that it took him some time to realise that the Goblin King wasn't big at all. In fact, he was small, very small. Tiny. He was so tiny that Raven Boy was looking down at him.

Then he spoke.

'So!' he squeaked in the squeakiest voice Raven Boy had ever heard. 'You're the one who's trying to kill me, are you?'

Raven Boy didn't know whether to laugh or cry. So he did both, and then he fainted.

TWELVE

Now, if there's one thing you ought to know about the Goblin King, it's this: he's the grumpiest thing on the planet. But don't ever tell him that.

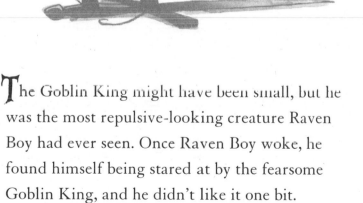

The Goblin King might have been small, but he was the most repulsive-looking creature Raven Boy had ever seen. Once Raven Boy woke, he found himself being stared at by the fearsome Goblin King, and he didn't like it one bit.

As well as being ugly, the Goblin King had a really, really mean look on his face.

'So!' he sneered. 'You think you can just sneak in here with your friends and kill me, do you?'

Raven Boy was shaking so hard he found it hard to speak.

'We don't have to kill you,' said Raven Boy.

The Goblin King seemed to be amused by that idea.

'Oh yeah?' he squeaked. 'And why wouldn't you? You seem to be armed to the teeth with swords and bows and . . . carpets.'

'We wouldn't have to,' said Raven Boy, 'if you agreed to stop invading the world and bring all your goblin armies back.'

The Goblin King stared at Raven Boy, and his mouth slowly dropped open. Then he burst out laughing.

'Ridiculous!' he snorted. 'Stop invading! Why would I stop? I'm about to take over the whole world with my nasty little goblins and there's no way I'm about to stop!'

Raven Boy shivered in his boots as the Goblin King stomped about in front of him.

'B-but . . . why?' asked Raven Boy.

'Why what?' snapped the evil gobbling ruler.

'Why do you want to take over the world?'

'Why?' roared the Goblin King, if it's possible to roar in a tiny squeaky voice. 'Why?'

'Yes. Why?'

The Goblin King got so mad at this point that Raven Boy wondered if he might just explode from crossness. He hoped he would, because maybe then they could all go home.

Elf Girl waved down at Raven Boy from her cage, trying to make him feel braver than he was. It didn't work. The trolls gave him a big thumbs-up. That didn't work either.

'Why?' squeaked the Goblin King again.

'Yes. Why?'

'I'll tell you why!' said his evil ugliness.

'Because I want to! That's why!'

'That's not a reason,' said Raven Boy.

'Yes it is!' squealed the Goblin King. 'It is if I say it is, see? I've had enough of people like you. You always know best, don't you? Always looking down on me, aren't you? Never take me seriously, do you? Well, you'll take me seriously now!'

On and on the Goblin King went, stomping about as he ranted and raved. Raven Boy noticed something, something that the Goblin King wasn't saying.

'Excuse me,' said Raven Boy.

The Goblin King stared at him.

'What?'

'Oh, I don't know really,' said Raven Boy. 'I was just wondering how someone as little as you can be so angry . . .'

Elf Girl winced.

Even the trolls hid their faces behind

their big fat hairy hands and Rat ducked out of sight in Klingsor's cloak. If anyone had looked closely, they would have even seen the carpet trembling as it lay rolled up on the floor.

Raven Boy thought he could see steam coming out of the Goblin King's ears and then the ugly little beast jumped up and down on the spot.

'I am not little!' he screeched. 'Don't you ever say that again! I'm going to kill you and then bring you back to life and then kill you all over again! That's just like your type! Always looking down on me. Well, that's all going to end when I rule the world!'

Raven Boy put his hand up to ask another question.

'Excuse me,' he said. 'Are you saying you're trying to take over the world just because . . . just because . . . you're really, I mean, really . . . short?'

Elf Girl mouthed the words 'oh no' and then fainted.

Socket's hair curled in fright then straightened again.

Klingsor tried to hide in his cloak with Rat.

The trolls all hugged each other, wishing they'd never left their home in Fright Forest. Cedric gave Raven Boy a thumbs-down sign and then hid his eyes.

Raven Boy blinked, waiting for some kind of answer from the Goblin King, but all he did was turn away, waving his hands at some of the goblins nearby.

'Lock them up while I think of the most painful way to kill them all,' he said. 'And throw their stuff in the lava.'

Then the Goblin King marched off again, back the way he'd come, with steam coming out of his ears.

Rough goblin hands grabbed Raven Boy, as the others were lowered from the ceiling. Their hands were tied behind their backs and they were dragged away.

As they went, they just had time to see a goblin pick up the Singing Sword, and throw it into a pit of molten lava.

'No!' yelled Raven Boy.

Then, after it, went the Tears of the Moon.

'No!' screeched Elf Girl.

And, with their eyes wide open in horror, they saw another goblin pick up the carpet, and send it down into the pit too.

'Nooo! Shona!' they screamed, and began to try and fight their way free, but it was no use.

Very soon, they were shoved into a small cave with iron railings across the entrance, and locked in by a big goblin with a fat metal key. They sat down, and thought about Shona, and even though she hadn't always been particularly good company, they were very sad indeed.

THIRTEEN

**Lord Socket got to be Lord
Socket because his dad was
Lord Socket before him.
That, plus the fact he's really
good at being snooty.**

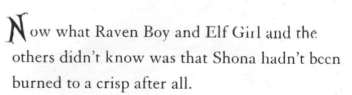

Now what Raven Boy and Elf Girl and the
others didn't know was that Shona hadn't been
burned to a crisp after all.

It seemed as though the goblins had
thrown her, and the sword and the tears, into
the lava pit, but in fact they had dropped them
onto a ledge just below, out of sight. Here, three
more goblins had caught the things and were
now carrying them away to the Goblin King's

secret museum, his collection of magical objects from around the world.

The goblins put the sword inside a glass case to try and muffle the sound of its singing. Then they put the Tears of the Moon on a shelf with a label that said 'Magical Water: powers unknown' and finally they hung Shona on a wall like a tapestry, though she decided not to let them know there was more to her than met the eye.

Then the goblins locked the museum, and stomped away, leaving the room in total darkness.

Meanwhile, Elf Girl and Raven Boy and the others were feeling very sorry for themselves indeed.

Raven Boy was trying to get Rat to come out of Klingsor's coat, but Rat refused.

'He's so scared he can't move his paws,' said Raven Boy.

'We're all that scared,' said Elf Girl. 'Even them,' she added, looking at the trolls, who were snivelling in the corner of the cell.

'And to think we used to be scared of you!' said Elf Girl.

'Well, you oughta be,' said Bert. 'We're still gonna eat you when all this is over.'

'Are we?' said Bob.

'I fink so,' said Cedric.

'Look, can we please not bring that up again?' asked Raven Boy.

Elf Girl turned to the trolls.

'Will you please stop crying? You big babies!'

'But we've come all this way,' said Bert. 'And now we won't get what we came for!'

'Yes,' said Raven Boy, looking puzzled, 'what was that anyway?'

Bert looked at Bob and Cedric looked at Bert and they all shrugged.

'We may as well tell 'im,' they all said at once.

'We came here,' Bob explained, 'to get the mys-tic-al thingy of wotsit.'

Bert knocked Bob on the top of his head.

'We came 'ere to get the mystical ring of power,' he said.

'The what?' asked Socket.

'The mystical ring of power. A magical ring with the power to stop us from turning into trolls.'

Raven Boy and Elf Girl stared at Bert.

'And you think the Goblin King has it?'

'We know he does,' said Bert. 'He has this secret museum, see? Only it's not so secret because we bashed the news out of a goblin we met last year. And in the museum, he has all sorts of magical things. Including—'

'The mys-tic-al thingy of wotsit!' cried Cedric.

Bert slapped his forehead, but he nodded.

'That's right,' he said.

'So that's why you came along with us!' said Raven Boy. 'To get the ring and turn yourselves back into men for good!'

'No,' said Bert.

'No?' asked Raven Boy.

'No,' said Bert. 'We like being trolls. What we hate is turning into trolls every night. It really hurts! If we get the ring, it can make us trolls all the time. See?'

Raven Boy shook his head in wonder.

'You lot are very stupid,' he said.

'Not really,' said Bob. 'We make really ugly men, but trolls are supposed to be ugly. We're much happier that way.'

'Yeah,' said Cedric. 'And bashing stuff is fun too.'

Elf Girl put her hand on Raven Boy's shoulder.

'There's really no arguing with that,' she said. 'They're smarter than they look.'

'Well, I never,' said Klingsor. 'The mystical ring of power.'

'Well, you're not the only ones who wanted to be something else,' said Socket.

'Whassat?' said Bert.

'You're not the only ones who aren't happy as you are. That carpet. Shona. She was once just a normal girl, but then she got stuck as a carpet.'

Everyone stared at Socket then.

'How do you know?' asked Elf Girl.

'She told me,' Socket said.

'You had a conversation with her?'

Socket nodded.

'Wow,' said Elf Girl. 'You must have been the only person ever.'

'Oh yes,' said Socket. 'She wanted to be a girl again, not a carpet. That's why she was cross all the time.'

'Well, I could have helped her with that,' said Klingsor. 'I wish I'd known. A simple spell to break, that one.'

And then the friends were sad again, thinking about Shona, and how all she wanted was to be normal.

Just like the trolls. Well, sort of.

FOURTEEN

**Have you ever tried to
wash a troll? Don't! It
always goes badly, and
someone gets hurt in the
process.**

Not too far away, down some of the tiny twisting
tunnels of the Creepy Caves, Shona the carpet
had been having an interesting time. She'd been
hanging on the wall, minding her own business,
and wondering if she could fly off the hooks
she was on. From time to time, the two nasty
goblins who'd put her there came back, and
muttered about this and that. They seemed very
interested in the new items in the Goblin King's

museum: the sword, the tears and her.

'We have to find out about them,' said one goblin to the other.

'You think I don't know that?' replied the other goblin. 'If he comes down here and we can't tell him what they are and how they work, we'll be on the menu by supper time.'

The first goblin gave a funny squeak, which Shona could have sworn sounded like 'Eep!', but she knew that only Raven Boy made such silly sounds. And Elf Girl, sometimes.

Still, it did seem that the two goblins who looked after the museum were very, very worried about something, and that something seemed to be the fact that the Goblin King was bound to come down to his collection of magical objects sooner or later, and when he did, a mild roasting of their bottoms would be the least they would suffer. Unless they could find out how everything worked.

The goblins inspected the sword in its glass case.

It was singing a song about how much rabbits love each other. For the fifteenth time in a row.

'This thing . . .' said the first goblin. 'It's doin' me 'ead in.'

The second goblin nodded.

'There must be some super dangerous power about it, or that boy with all the feathers wouldn't have brought it here to try and kill the King.'

'What about this?' asked the second goblin, staring at the Tears of the Moon.

The tears were just sitting on a shelf, looking like nothing more exciting than a small bottle of water.

They peered closely at it, and then both looked at each other.

'I s'pose you just drink it,' said the first goblin.

'No! It might be poison. You oughtn't to just drink anything when you don't know what it is! Don't you know nothin'?'

'Well, I'll just drink a bit, then.'

The second goblin thought about this for a while, then he nodded.

'Good idea,' he said.

Shona held her breath, wondering what would happen to the goblin when he drank from the bottle.

The nasty red monster glanced up the passageway then, seeing that the coast was clear, picked the bottle off the shelf, pulled out the cork, and gave it a quick sniff. Then he took a quick sip from the bottle and shoved it back on the shelf.

He turned to his friend.

'Well?' he said. 'Is I any different?'

'You haven't learned to speak proper,' the second goblin said. 'Apart from that, you don't look any different.'

The first goblin frowned. 'Maybe I've got some kind of super powers now,' he said. 'Hit me.'

'Do what?' said the second goblin.

'Hit me. See if I'm tougher than I was before.'

The second goblin shrugged and then smacked his friend on the nose, who went flying backwards.

'Don't think so,' said the second goblin.

His friend came back rubbing his nose.

'That 'urt,' he said.

'You told me to.'

'Never mind that. What about this rug?'

Shona froze to the wall, terrified they would find her out. She shivered as they came up really close and prodded her.

The first goblin laughed.

'That rug,' he said, 'is just a rug.'

'Yeah, but that lot outside said they saw it flying.'

'Right,' said the first goblin. 'But that lot outside are off their heads on hog-hooch 'alf the time, aren't they? Flying carpets! I ask you!'

'Yeah,' said the second goblin. 'I fink you're right. Let's get out of here for now, eh? That sword is doing me 'ead in.'

'Oh, I dunno,' said the first goblin as they wandered away. 'It's not so bad.'

They went off down the tunnel.

'Not so bad?' said the first one. 'Maybe I hit you on the nose too hard and your brain got knocked into your ear'oles?'

'Get off of it!' said his friend, and away they went.

Shona breathed a huge sigh of relief. She wondered what to do. She was fairly sure she could fly off the hooks she'd been hung on, but there were regulations about carpets flying themselves. Shona didn't much like having been turned into a flying air service, but she was one for rules, and if she had to be a carpet, she was at least going to stick to the laws of the sky. One of the first things she'd learned was that carpets do not fly themselves unattended, without passengers.

'Rules, Shona,' she said aloud. 'Rules.'

But then she took a peek at the cave, and she thought about the people she'd met, locked up who knows where in some horrible place, waiting to be executed by the Goblin King. There was the feather boy and the pointy girl. That rat who nibbled her tassels when no one was looking. The three smelly, not to say heavy, trolls. The crotchety old wizard. He wasn't so bad. And then there was that young, rich lord. He'd even spoken to her. Quite nicely.

Suddenly she felt a tear welling up in her

eye, and then she shouted, 'Stuff the rules!' and flew up off the hooks, speeding away down the tunnel as fast as she dared.

FIFTEEN

Raven Boy has also decided
that if he ever gets home in
one piece, he's going to take
up a nice safe hobby, like
flower arranging.

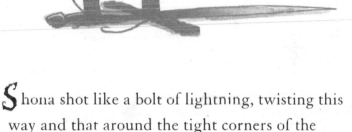

Shona shot like a bolt of lightning, twisting this
way and that around the tight corners of the
tunnels of the Creepy Caves.

Once or twice she had some close calls;
she nearly ran into the back of a column
of marching goblins, and she found herself
speeding through the goblin kitchens, right
behind the goblin cook when his back was
turned.

Then, worst of all, she found that she
had shot out into a vast cavern and was high in
the air. She heard voices below her and looked
down to see the Goblin King himself stomping
around, shouting at his chiefs.

'You are going to take over the whole
world by tea-time or else!' he cried.

'Or else what, mighty Goblin King?'
asked one of his chiefs, who was smart enough
to slip the word 'mighty' into his question.

'Or else you won't believe how much trouble you'll be in!' squealed the Goblin King.

'Ooh,' said one chief.

And 'Eeee!' said another.

'That does sound bad,' agreed a third and fourth goblin chief. 'We'll do our best.'

'Your best!' spluttered the Goblin King. 'You can stuff that with pickles! Either the whole world is in my hands by tea-time, or .'

He trailed off.

'Or what, o great one?' asked a chief.

'Never mind! Just do it!' screeched the Goblin King in his squeaky voice. 'Now! About these prisoners! I want a nasty way of killing them. Really nasty. So everyone gets the idea about how mean I am. So? Any ideas?'

The goblin chiefs all stared at each other, muttering and saying, 'You' and 'No, you' and then they all nudged one forward.

He blinked a couple of times.

'Well?' demanded the Goblin King.

'Erm,' said the chief. 'Um. Hurm. Um. You could get a feather, and tickle them to death.'

The Goblin King stared at him, speechless.

'And perhaps we could massage their shoulders while we do it? Idiot! Numbskull! Dimwit!'

The Goblin King kicked the chief in the shins. The chief seemed not to have noticed that he'd been kicked, but the Goblin King hopped about for a while, holding his toes.

'Anyone else?' he hissed, through his teeth.

'Well,' said another goblin chief, 'we could get some mice . . .'

Shona had had enough. As silently as she could, she slipped away before she could hear any more terrifying execution plans.

She was beginning to think she would never find where her friends had been locked up, but she sped on, knowing there was no time to waste.

'Tea time!' she said to herself. 'That's very soon! We have to save the world!'

For the first time ever, Shona found that she was thinking about someone else other than herself, and though she was a bit surprised by that, she decided she liked it.

Then, suddenly, she saw a small cave, with bars across it, and on a hunch, she sped towards it.

Inside were her friends. They made the most pitiful sight, all asleep, curled up on one another for warmth and comfort.

Raven Boy even had his thumb in his mouth, though that wasn't as bad as the trolls,

because Cedric had his thumb in Bob's mouth.

'Wake up!' Shona called, as loud as she dared.

No one moved. Even Rat was so tired from being scared all the time that not a whisker twitched as Shona called out a little louder.

No response.

'Wake up!' she almost screamed, and still none of them moved.

'Nothing else for it,' she said, and decided to perform a very tricky flying manoeuvre; to fly sideways through the bars of the cell.

It was tough, but she pulled it off neatly, and was only a bit sad that no one was awake to see it.

Once she was through, she flew straight at Raven Boy's head, waking him up immediately.

'Oh!' he wailed, seeing Shona in front of him. 'I'm dreaming! What a nightmare! Poor Shona!'

And he began to sniff so loudly that Elf Girl woke up too.

'You are not dreaming!' yelled Shona. 'You're awake, you numpty!'

'Awake! Then you're a ghost! Oh, Shona!'

And he buried his head in his hands as Elf Girl shrieked.

'Ghosts! Ghosts!'

This went on for some time, and Shona got very cross trying to wake everyone up and tell them that no, they weren't dreaming, and yes, she really was alive, and not a ghost.

Eventually, everyone was awake and understood the situation, even Cedric, though he'd had to get Bob to draw a picture in the dirt on the floor before he'd finally got it.

'Not dead? he said, looking at Shona.

'That's marvellous!' cried Socket, and tried to hug the carpet as she flew.

She took the hug, wincing a little.

'That was awkward,' whispered Raven Boy to Klingsor.

'I think he might be in love with Shona,' said the wizard.

'In love with a carpet!' spluttered Raven Boy.

'I am not!' said Socket, stepping away from Shona.

Shona stared at him.

'Well,' said Socket. 'I mean. I'm in love with a girl.'

He beamed at Shona, like a sheepish goat. She stared back, like a goatish sheep.

'You what?' she said.

'If only you were a

real girl,' Socket sighed.

'Well,' said Klingsor. 'I told you. That's a spell that's easily broken. With a . . .'

'Wait!' cried Elf Girl. 'Don't do it!'

'Don't do it?' cried Socket.

'Don't do it?' asked Raven Boy.

'No!' said Elf Girl. 'If Shona's going to become a real girl again, don't you think it would be better if she did so outside the cell?'

'Oh,' said Klingsor. 'Good point!'

Sixteen

**That thing about Raven Boy
and flower arranging?
That's true.**

In a flash, Shona shot through the bars of the
cell, and this time got a small round of applause
from Socket for her nifty sideways trick.

She bobbed up and down, hovering and
shaking at the same time, as she waited for
Klingsor to break the spell that had turned her
into a flying carpet.

The magician was rummaging around
in his cloak and pulled out a small pouch, from

which he pulled some dirty and boring-looking wool.

'Is that to break the spell?' asked Elf Girl.

'No,' said Klingsor, 'it's for the noise.'

'What noise?' asked Raven Boy, as Klingsor stuffed the wool in his ears, and then muttered something while waving his hands towards the carpet.

There was the loudest bang any of them had ever heard, and a blinding flash of light and, when they opened their eyes again, there was Shona. The real Shona, standing on a very unmagical-looking rug.

She rushed to the bars and kissed Klingsor on the nose.

He pulled away, making a funny squawking sound, and then Socket stepped forward and knelt in front of Shona.

'Oh my dear,' he said.

'You are more beautiful than I could have imagined.'

Elf Girl and Raven Boy rolled their eyes at each other.

'I thought she'd be taller,' whispered Elf Girl.

'My love,' said Socket, who was still staring dreamily into Shona's eyes, 'would you do me the honour of becoming my wife?'

Shona giggled in a way that seemed to mean yes, and the trolls all cheered.

'This is all very lovely,' cried Raven Boy. 'But that was the loudest bang in history. Very soon this place is going to be full of goblins wanting to know what's going on. And we're still locked inside.'

'You are!' said Shona. 'But I'm not. And what you don't know is this . . .'

She danced over to the wall, where a big key was hanging on a hook.

'Careless goblins,' she said. 'Oh, it feels good to have real legs again.'

She skipped back to the bars and unlocked the gate to their cell.

'Come on! We have to stop the Goblin King!'

'We know that,' muttered Elf Girl. 'Whose adventure was this in the first place?'

Shona was in too good a mood to mind Elf Girl.

'What you don't know is that we don't have long. The Goblin King is going to invade the world by tea-time!'

'EEEP!' cried Raven Boy.

'That's the Raven Boy I know and love!' said Elf Girl, and then everyone stared at her.

Raven Boy blushed, but snuck a peek at Elf Girl.

'It's these two!' she said quickly, pointing at Socket and Shona. 'That's why I said it. Put the word in my head. When I say love, I mean . . .'

But though she tried to take it back, Raven Boy was still blushing.

Klingsor sighed.

'Young people!' he muttered. 'Come on. Bird boy is right. We have to get out of here. Now.'

'What about your carpet?' Socket asked Shona.

'Not mine any more. And no use to us, I'm afraid. It's now as magical as a wet sheep.'

'Then we're on foot from here,' said Raven Boy, and led the way down the corridor, while Shona told them all about the museum.

'Mu-se-um?' asked Cedric, who was lumbering along at the back.

'Museum!' said Bert. 'Shona, did you see a mystical ring of power in the museum?'

'I saw all sorts of things. He's got quite a collection of stuff.'

'Never mind that now,' said Elf Girl. 'We need the sword and the tears. And my bow!'

'We still don't know how they work,' said Raven Boy. 'The tears, I mean, and the sword.'

'Yes, well, I've been thinking about that,' said Klingsor, as Shona took over from Raven Boy and led the way back down the corridors towards the museum.

They made a few more turns and then, there it was. The Goblin King's museum.

It seemed to be deserted, but two torches on the wall illuminated the objects inside.

The gang rushed in, and Elf Girl grabbed her bow, and the tears.

The trolls were hunting around for the mystical thingy of wotsit, and Raven Boy stood by the glass case inside which was the sword, singing something about treetops and honeybees.

'I'll break the glass, and grab it, so it stops,' said Raven Boy.

'Very good,' said Klingsor.

'So what have you been thinking?' asked Elf Girl.

'I was trying to remember the rest of the prophecy about the wise fool.'

Raven Boy groaned.

'Not that again.'

'That again!' said Klingsor. 'It goes on for verse after verse, you know. I was trying to remember verses sixteen and seventeen.'

'Seventeen?' wailed Raven Boy.

'Yes,' said Klingsor, 'but they're not nearly as interesting as verse thirty-two.'

'Meep,' said Raven Boy.

'Why?' asked Elf Girl. 'What's so special about verse thirty-two?'

'Oh, just that in verse thirty-two, there's something about how the Goblin King can be destroyed by the Singing Sword, but only if he's drunk the Tears of the Moon first.'

'That's it!' cried Elf Girl. 'That's what we have to do! It's so easy!'

'Easy?' said Raven Boy, looking very worried.

'Yes! We get him to drink the tears, and then you can run in with the sword and chop his head off! Hooray!'

Raven Boy didn't look very happy.

'Hooray,' he said, in a tiny voice.

'Come on, Raven Boy,' said Elf Girl. 'This is your big moment! You can do it!'

'But how are we going to get him to drink the Tears of the Moon? Are you going to walk right up to him and see if he's thirsty?'

'No,' said Shona, 'But we could put in his soup . . .'

'And how are we going to do that?' asked Raven Boy. 'Do you know where the kitchens are?'

'Yes,' said Shona, 'I do.'

'So do I,' said Klingsor.

Rat popped his head out for the first time in a long while, and squeaked.

'You too?' sighed Raven Boy. 'Oh, goody.'

So that was that. They had a plan, and nothing Raven Boy could say would stop it.

SEVENTEEN

Elf Girl has been dreaming about lying on a sunny beach for a month. That's assuming they don't get killed by the fearsome Goblin King, of course.

Finding the kitchens was easy, too easy as far as Raven Boy was concerned, with Rat leading the way, his whiskers twitching like crazy.

'Supposing there's someone in the kitchens?' said Raven Boy.

'Good!' cried Bert. 'It's been far too long since we bashed anything!'

Bob and Cedric agreed and before anyone could stop them, they began playfully hitting

each other on the head, just for fun.

'And did you find the mystical ring of power?' asked Raven Boy, as casually as he could.

'Oh yeah!' said Bert. 'We did. And as soon as we work out how to use it, we'll be trolls forever!'

'You seem to have been trolls the whole time you've been down here,' said Raven Boy. 'Haven't you? And we must have been down here in daytime as well as night-time now.'

'That is true,' said Bob.

'If we don't see the sun we stay as trolls

anyway,' explained Bert.

'But we wanna be trolls the 'ole time, see?' added Cedric, helpfully.

Then they were in the kitchens.

It was as smelly and hot as when Shona had flown through it before, and Rat and Klingsor had been caught.

From behind a rock, they watched the goblin chef preparing a big pot of soup.

'That should keep him quiet for a while,' the chef muttered, and it was all Raven Boy and Elf Girl could do not to snigger. Then they thought about the horrible ways the Goblin King was going to kill them and they shut up.

The chef put the soup into a little bowl with a little spoon on a tray with a glass of lemon squash.

'There!' hissed Elf Girl. 'His juice! We just need to sneak up and . . .'

Her words faded as she saw the three trolls march out into the kitchen and bash the goblin chef so hard on the head that he passed out.

'There ya go,' said Bert, and waved a hand to show Elf Girl it was safe to come out.

She tiptoed out into the kitchen and poured half the bottle of the tears into the Goblin King's soup, and then the other half into his lemon squash.

'Fingers crossed,' she said, but then she thought of something. She turned to the trolls, who were looking much happier for getting to do some bashing. 'Who's going to take it to him? Now you've bashed the chef on the bonce?'

They all thought about that, and no one had any good ideas. Then they heard footsteps coming towards the kitchen, and they all ran and hid. The trolls dragged the chef out of sight, just as a weasely orange goblin stuck his head into the kitchen.

'Where's that fat lump got to?' he said. Then he saw the tray of food, and shrugged.

He came over, sniffed the air a couple of times, suspiciously, and then shrugged again. He picked the tray up, and went back down the tunnel.

'Old Gobbly King is going to have his wemonade,' he said, chuckling to himself, as he went.

'You know,' said Raven Boy, as they all stood up from their hiding places again. 'No one actually seems to like their King very much, do they?'

'I know the feeling,' said Socket.

'Well, you were very mean to everyone in Little Nicely, weren't you?' Elf Girl pointed out.

'Not any more,' said Socket. 'When I return, I will be the kindest ruler anywhere ever had. With the most beautiful ruleress.'

He winked at Shona, who giggled.

'Oh, for goodness' sake,' said Elf Girl.

They decided to follow the orange goblin, at a safe distance, towards the Goblin King's hall. Once they saw him drink the juice, or taste the soup, while Elf Girl used her bow and the trolls used their fists to keep the other goblins away, Raven Boy would run out with the sword and lop the Goblin King's head off.

That was the plan. Raven Boy thought it sucked, but no one was listening to him, so he just went along with everyone else, the Singing Sword gripped tightly in his hand.

'Hot in here,' whispered Elf Girl, who was near the front.

'Yes, hot,' agreed Klingsor behind her.

''Ot,' said the trolls, and Socket nodded.

'Hot, isn't?' he whispered to Raven Boy, who was at the back.

'EEP,' said Raven Boy. 'Hot. Very hot.'

'Heh heh heh,' said a voice behind Raven Boy. 'It'll be even hotter soon.'

'Why's that?' asked Raven Boy, turning round. Then he saw why. There were around a hundred goblins all sneaking down the corridor, just behind him.

'Oh, nuts,' Raven Boy said.

'You'll be hot once we roast you over a nice lava pit,' said the goblin behind him, and then there were goblins all over them, swarming around them and overpowering even the trolls.

Very soon, they were back in front of the Goblin King, who was so mad it looked like he might explode on the spot.

'You have crossed me for the last time!' he squealed, and no one could think of anything to say to that, apart from Raven Boy, who said 'Eeep,' once, though his heart wasn't really in it.

EIGHTEEN

Rat worries about Raven Boy and Elf Girl a lot. Which is very sensible, because Raven Boy and Elf Girl are in very great danger. All the time.

The hall of the Goblin King was full of goblins.

They crowded around the prisoners, who were each held by a strong goblin, or two in the case of the trolls.

Another goblin had snatched the sword from Raven Boy, so it was singing again, and another had snatched Elf Girl's bow.

The Goblin King was stomping around, looking furious, as furious as if someone had

told him what all his Christmas presents were
and spoiled the surprise.

On a low rock wall nearby were his
tray of soup and glass of lemonade. Both were
untouched, something that Elf Girl and Raven
Boy had not failed to notice.

'So then!' screeched the Goblin King.
'How shall I kill you? All the same way or a
different way for each of you?'

'You really don't have to kill us,' tried
Raven Boy. 'And then we don't have to kill you
and we can all be nice to each other and . . .'

'Will someone shut that boy up?'
screeched the Goblin King and Raven Boy felt a
hand cover his mouth. It was hairy and it smelt.

'Let me explain something,' the Goblin
King said to Raven Boy, coming close and
peering up at him. 'I am going to be ruler of
the world by tea-time, and nothing and no one
is going to stop me.'

'Mmmm-mmmf,' said Raven Boy.

'What?' asked the Goblin King.

The hand disappeared from Raven Boy's
mouth.

'I said, are you sure?' said Raven Boy.

'Yes, I'm sure,' snapped the Goblin King, and the hand clamped over Raven Boy's mouth again.

'Can we get on and kill this lot?' wailed the Goblin King.

'Any time you like,' said one of his chiefs.

'Good! Very good!' he cried. 'Do it now! Throw them in the river of lava! I've had enough!'

The goblins began to drag the gang of friends towards the edge of the river, when suddenly the Goblin King shouted.

'Stop! Wait! I'm thirsty and I want my lemonade first.'

Raven Boy shot a look at Elf Girl, and she raised her eyebrows.

They looked at Klingsor, who nodded to the trolls, and then, while they held their breath, the Goblin King stomped over to the tray like a stroppy toddler, and drank the whole glass of lemonade in one go.

Before anyone could do anything else, Klingsor muttered some magic words, and the goblins holding the three trolls suddenly thought their tails were on fire and began hopping about, trying to put them out.

The trolls wasted no time, and began bashing anything that looked even a bit like a goblin.

Bert rushed up to the goblin holding Elf Girl's bow and bopped him on the head, while

Bob did the same to the one holding the sword, and threw it to Raven Boy, who snatched it from the floor.

'Stop them!' squealed the Goblin King, and goblins began to rush in from all sides. Elf Girl fired her bow, again and again, and every shot was a good one, sending out small thunderbolts that took out five goblins at once.

'Quick!' yelled Elf Girl. 'Cut his head off!'

Raven Boy swallowed hard.

The Goblin King was hopping around, mad as a brush, screaming at his goblins to kill them. Raven Boy thought about everyone at home, all the badgers, and the robins. He thought about everyone they'd met on their way, some of them grumpy, some of them very helpful. And he thought about Elf Girl and how much he wanted to stay being her friend.

He swallowed again, and then ran towards the Goblin King, waving the sword above his head, yelling.

Then he tripped on the floor of the cave and the sword went flying up in the air, and then landed, point first, sticking itself into the rock.

It began to sing.

'I like the little fishes,
in the sea,
they look so cute,
like you and me . . .'

'Nooo!' wailed Elf Girl. 'Get it!'

Bob was by the sword, trying to pull it out and give it to Raven Boy again, but the sword was stuck fast. It would not move.

Despite this, it kept up its song, moving into a second verse, this one about how sweet baby deer are.

Rat had heard the singing and jumped onto Raven Boy's head. He was swaying and dancing and trying to squeak along to the singing, and then Raven Boy noticed something.

Just as Rat was dancing, so was the Goblin King. He had stopped screaming and shouting and, far from having one of his tantrums, was dancing on one foot, trying to sing along to the sword's song, even though he didn't know the words.

'Look!' said Raven Boy, and everyone stopped, even the goblins, who stared at their leader in amazement.

'Look there, too!' said Elf Girl, who had seen that a couple of the other goblins were doing the same thing; dancing about with dreamy looks on their faces. One of them was the goblin who'd carried the 'wemonade' and

another, Shona pointed out, was the goblin who
ran the museum.

'He drank from the bottle!' she cried.
'He drank some of the tears!'

Raven Boy turned to Rat.

'Rat?' he asked. 'Is there something you
never told us? About when we went to the oasis
and found the Tears of the Moon?'

Rat squeaked at Raven Boy for a while,
though Elf Girl could tell that even Raven

Boy was having a hard time understanding his rodent friend.

'I think,' said Raven Boy, 'I think he's saying that he drank from the oasis, too. Klingsor, this thing, in verse thirty-two of the prophecy? Are you sure it says the Goblin King can be "destroyed" by the sword, once he's drunk the tears?'

Klingsor thought hard.

'Maybe,' he said. 'Although it might have been "delighted",' he added.

Raven Boy laughed.

'That's it!' he cried. 'Look! Whoever drinks the tears adores the Singing Sword's dreadful singing!'

'But what about the other goblins?' asked Elf Girl. The other goblins, as she put it, weren't fighting them any more. They weren't doing anything but watching their King make a fool of himself. Right now he was trying to dance with Bert, who was having none of it.

'Hooray!' said Raven Boy. 'We've done it!'

'Aren't you going to chop his head off?' asked Shona.

'No,' said Raven Boy very firmly. 'That's not very nice, is it? And if I've learned one thing from all our adventures, it's that the world would be a better place if everyone was nicer.'

Here, he looked hopefully at the trolls, who had, after all, still promised to eat them once this adventure was over.

Bert stared at Raven Boy.

'We'll think about it,' he said, but he winked.

NINETEEN

Saving the world might have been scary at times, but it's made Raven Boy and Elf Girl and Rat into the very best friends.

It didn't take long to sort things out, but they got sorted out in a way that Raven Boy and Elf Girl never would have imagined.

It seemed that what Klingsor had said was true; goblins do whatever their leader tells them.

So when they got the Goblin King to tell his goblins that he wasn't their ruler any more, they all agreed to that straightaway. The Goblin King didn't seem to mind; he was busy listening to the sword, and had a dreamy look on his face. He agreed to anything and everything that was suggested to him, and his last act as ruler was to call off the attack on the rest of the world.

'What do we do with him now?' asked Elf Girl.

'I've got an idea,' said Klingsor. 'You don't want to walk home all that way, do you?'

'No,' said Raven Boy. 'But the carpet's not magic any more.'

He glared at Shona and Socket, who were being lovey-dovey in the corner, discussing what colour to paint their castle when they got back, and how many children they'd have.

'Three!' said Shona.

'Yes!' agreed Socket. 'One of each!'

Everyone looked at him strangely, and Raven Boy felt like pulling his feathers out.

'See? Shona's no use any more.'

'No, but the carpet is. All it needs is a new pilot.'

Klingsor smiled at the Goblin King.

A while later, the Goblin King, who was king no more, but was jigging about to the sound of the sword, didn't even notice as

Klingsor made a magic spell and turned him
into the new pilot of the flying carpet.

'What about that?' asked Elf Girl, but
Raven Boy had an idea.

'Boys, could you help me?' he asked, and
the trolls came over. Between the three of them,
they managed to pull the sword from the rock,
and handed it to Raven Boy.

'No one minds, do they?' he asked, dangling
it over the lava pit.

Rat squeaked angrily, but no one else
minded, as Raven Boy dropped the sword into
the lava, where it melted almost immediately,
halfway through a line about bunny rabbits.

At once, the pilot of the carpet was a stroppy goblin again, but one who could do nothing except what he was told.

And the first place he was told to fly was Terror Town, now known once more as Little Nicely. But before that, there was something odd that happened.

'What's to stop this lot turning nasty?' asked Socket, waving his hands at the now leaderless goblin hordes.

'What they need is a new ruler,' said Klingsor. 'Or three . . .'

He looked at the trolls.

'How about it, chaps? You could keep this lot in order, couldn't you? I'll tell you how the mystical ring of power works – not that you'll need it if you stay here. As rulers . . .'

The trolls looked at each other.

'Rulers?' said Bob.

'In charge?' asked Cedric.

'Top dogs?' said Bert.

'Top trolls,' said Klingsor.

'Done! We'll take the job,' said Bert.

'And no eating anyone?' asked Raven Boy.

'No promises,' said Bert. 'That's our best offer.'

'Okay,' said Raven Boy. 'Deal. Well? Shall we go?'

And they did, and they even gave the trolls a hug, though it was a pretty quick hug, just in case they changed their minds about eating them.

They climbed onto the carpet, told the goblin to go, and they were off, back to Little Nicely.

'Goodbye, trolls,' cried Raven Boy.

They waved, and the trolls waved back. Cedric seemed to be wiping a tear from his eyes, but even before they were out of sight, they saw Bert bashing goblins about, just to remind them who was in charge.

At Little Nicely, the carpet set down Klingsor, Shona and Socket. Shona and Socket

were all over each other, and barely noticed that Elf Girl and Raven Boy were leaving. Klingsor went off muttering that he was going to resign as a wizard, and then the carpet flew on.

The flight was long, and they flew over desert and sea, and across high snowy mountains, past dragons, and genies, and pirates and zombies, until finally they saw the trees of their home coming towards them.

Rat ran around in circles as they swooped into the comforting sight of their wood, with new trees springing up in place of the ones the ogre had knocked down.

Then, Elf Girl saw her family ahead of her, waving and cheering.

'We did it!' she cried, and they began to laugh and cry at the same time.

The carpet landed and everyone hugged Raven Boy and Elf Girl, and there and then they decided to throw a huge party to celebrate, a party that went on long into the night.

While everyone was eating and dancing and drinking and laughing, Elf Girl and Raven Boy sneaked away. It was wonderful to be home, but strange too.

'It's so noisy!' said Raven Boy. 'It used to be quiet in the woods.'

'Yes, it was,' agreed Elf Girl. 'Until you fell through my roof.'

Raven Boy laughed.

'Sorry about that,' he said.

'I forgive you.'

They were quiet for a while, and then Elf Girl said, quietly, 'So, Raven Boy, what are you, um, I mean, where will you . . . I mean . . .'

Raven Boy interrupted her.

'Will I see you again?' he asked.

Elf Girl smiled, blushing.

'Yes. Will you see me again?'

'I was thinking,' said Raven Boy. 'You need a new hut, don't you?'

'I do,' said Elf Girl.

'And I need a new tree to live in. Maybe I could find a nice tree, and we could build you a new hut right at the bottom of it. And then we could see each other whenever we wanted.'

'All the time!' said Elf Girl.

Raven Boy grinned.

'Yes, all the time.'

They laughed, because it was good to be home, and they were happy, and then Elf Girl remembered something.

She sat bolt upright and jabbed a finger into Raven Boy's chest.

'Tell me!' she demanded.

'Nope,' said Raven Boy, shaking his head.

'You said you would.'

'I said maybe I would.'

Elf Girl's ears began to turn pink.

'Reginald!'

'No,' said Raven Boy.

'Randall?'

'Uh-uh.'

'Russell.'

'Oh!' said Raven Boy.

'I got it?' asked Elf Girl, her eyes widening.

'No,' said Raven Boy, winking. 'Nowhere near.'

'Raven Boy!' screeched Elf Girl, and so

they went on, and on and on, until finally Elf
Girl realised that she didn't even mind if she
didn't know Raven Boy's real name, because
what mattered was that she'd found a real
friend, for life.

If you enjoyed Creepy Caves you'll love Marcus Sedgwick's other series for younger readers,

THE RAVEN MYSTERIES.

Meet Valevine the inventor, Minty who was once a witch, gorgeous, glum Solstice, her little brother Cudweed and his monkey, Fellah, and Edgar the raven, their self-appointed Guardian.

'Nobody likes a sticky monkey'

Edgar's alarmed when a nasty looking black tail
slinks off under the rhubarb, kitchen maids go
missing and the castle begins to flood. It won't be
long before the Otherhands come face to face with
the owner of the black tail.

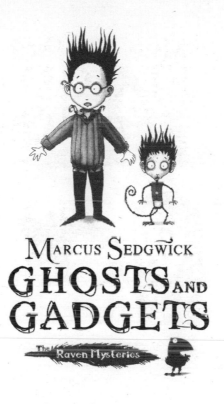

MARCUS SEDGWICK
GHOSTS AND GADGETS

The Raven Mysteries

'Does my beak look wonky?'

Edgar is so preoccupied that when Cudweed sees a
guh . . . a guh . . . You-Know-What, Edgar almost
forgets that he's the Guardian of Otherhand Castle.
But the rumblings and wailing from the Lost South
Wing can no longer be ignored. It's up to Solstice
and Edgar to go ghost-hunting, and pit their wits
against the obnoxious Captain Spookini.

MARCUS SEDGWICK
LUNATICS
AND LUCK
The Raven Mysteries

'This sort of stuff can bend your brain fairly rapidly.'

Full moons and money troubles are nothing out of
the ordinary at Castle Otherhand. But add a
horrible, hairy, howling new school teacher,
complete with mysterious heavy wooden trunk, and
the earth trembles and the body count rises.
Solstice and Cudweed are at his mercy. Gasp!

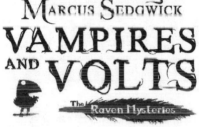

'Pumpkin brains everywhere!'

It's Halloween and the Otherhands are throwing a
Vampire Party . . . in the midst of which, the lights
go out, and the ballroom is plunged into darkness.
What happens next could only happen to them!
Thank goodness Edgar is there to swoop to the
rescue.

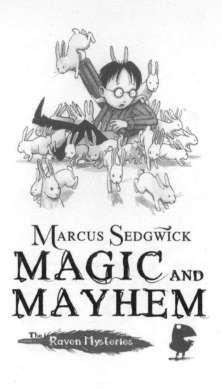

MARCUS SEDGWICK
MAGIC AND
MAYHEM

The Raven Mysteries

'A bored bird is a dangerous bird'

Following a family outing to the circus, Minty falls
under the spell of a dodgy fortune-teller, Castle
Otherhand is overrun by furry white bunnies, a
mucky duck and a hamster called Mr Whiskers, and
Valevine creates a strangely lethal cabbage-counting
contraption. Rark! The Castle is in mayhem.